Khalil and Mr. Hagerty and the Backyard Treasures

Tricia Springstubb

illustrated by
Elaheh Taherian

CANDLEWICK PRESS

Khalil's new house had an up and a down.

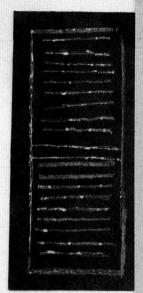

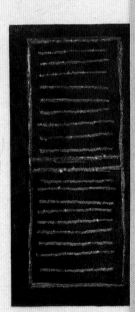
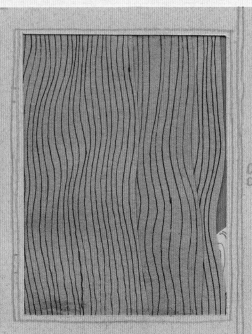

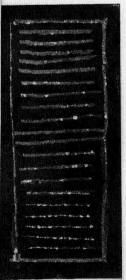

Upstairs lived his family, which was big and busy and noisy.

Downstairs lived Mr. Hagerty, who was quiet.

Khalil loved the backyard. So did Mr. Hagerty.

While Mr. Hagerty worked in his garden,
Khalil hunted for bugs and interesting rocks.

He lay in the grass and read his library books.

Sometimes, if he couldn't figure out a word, he asked for help. Mr. Hagerty would squint through his glasses.

"Tarantula," Mr. Hagerty would say quietly.

Or "Volcano."

Or "Doubloons."

Sometimes, Mr. Hagerty needed help with his words, too.

"Where did I put my . . . my digging thing, my hole maker . . . my . . ."

"Shovel?"

"Look at this big . . . not beeper, not beastie . . ."

"Beetle?"

That summer, the house was hot. Upstairs and downstairs, it was much too hot. Even in the backyard, the sun burned and the air sizzled.

One morning when Khalil went out, everything looked droopy.
Even Mr. Hagerty.

Khalil decided this would be a
good day to find buried treasure.

The ground was hard to dig. Khalil found a few things, but not what anyone would call treasure.

Mr. Hagerty dug, too. He found some carrots, but they were small and shriveled.

The word for this was *discouraging*.

"We need refreshments," said Mr. Hagerty.

Refreshments turned out to mean big pieces of chocolate cake and tall, cold glasses of milk.

Soon, Khalil and Mr. Hagerty both felt much better.

"Maybe we'll be luckier tomorrow," said Khalil.

"Maybe," said Mr. Hagerty.

Upstairs that night, Khalil had an idea.

Downstairs, so did Mr. Hagerty.

First thing in the morning, Khalil raced down into the yard.

Mr. Hagerty was already there. He looked excited. As excited as Khalil.

"You better get digging," he said, and his voice was not the least bit quiet.

"You too," said Khalil.

This was when something wonderful happened.

Two somethings.

No sooner did Mr. Hagerty put his shovel in the dirt than he dug up a big, juicy carrot.

That would have been wonderful enough.
But then Khalil found buried treasure!

"This calls for refreshments!" he said.

They celebrated with carrot sticks and chocolate cake.

"It's our lucky day," said Khalil.

"Lucky's the word," said Mr. Hagerty.

That night, as Khalil looked out
his window upstairs, he thought
of another word. A very good
word. One of the best words
of all.

Downstairs, so did Mr. Hagerty.

Friend.

For my good friends
Khalil, Mohammed, Fatima, and Adam

T. S.

To all the children, around the world,
who are in search of safety and peace

E.T.

Text copyright © 2020 by Tricia Springstubb
Illustrations copyright © 2020 by Elaheh Taherian

First edition 2020

Library of Congress Catalog Card Number pending
ISBN 978-1-5362-0306-6

20 21 22 23 24 25 LEO 10 9 8 7 6 5 4 3 2 1

Printed in Heshan, Guangdong, China

This book was typeset in Gill Sans.
The illustrations were done in collage with oil and colored pencil.

Candlewick Press
99 Dover Street
Somerville, Massachusetts 02144

visit us at www.candlewick.com